Elias and the Dragon

Written by Jared Hunt

CARAMEL TREE

CHAPTER *1*

The King's Messenger

"One hundred gold pieces!" The old man's voice carried clearly across Gallive Village Square. "To the person who brings me the dragon's head."

Elias gasped along with the crowd of villagers that had gathered to hear the king's messenger. One hundred gold pieces! That was more money than the whole village had put together. But slaying a dragon?

Before he could think too hard about it, Elias was interrupted by a strong, bold voice. "Only one dragon? Where might I find the beast?" Elias watched as his older

brother, Lucas, pushed through the crowd of villagers.

'Of course,' Elias thought to himself, *'Lucas has been dreaming of this moment his whole life.'*

The king's messenger turned slowly to face Lucas, and Elias noticed a sly grin creep across his old wrinkled face. "It does not surprise me that Gallive would have a champion worthy of this task. What is your name, my good man?" asked the king's messenger.

"Lucas. Soon to be Lucas Dragon-slayer!" said Lucas as he raised a fist in salute to the crowd. The villagers laughed and nearby men clapped Lucas on his back. Unlike most of the men who cut their hair short, Lucas had long blonde hair and the morning sun made it shine.

"Indeed," replied the king's messenger. He looked Lucas up and down for a moment, observing his broad shoulders, muscular arms and tree-trunk legs. "Yes, I think you might be just the right person for the job." The king's messenger grinned.

"Just tell me where to find the dragon," said Lucas confidently as he patted the long dagger on his belt.

"Why do you want the dragon's head?" blurted Elias without thinking. Everyone in the crowd turned at once to face him. Elias felt blood rushing to his face and wished he could disappear.

"Come here, boy," commanded the king's messenger, pointing to the ground in front of him.

"Pay no attention to the boy," said Lucas angrily. "He's just a spoiled brat who hasn't learned to be silent when adults are speaking."

Elias moved forward slowly, his eyes focused on the ground. The crowd had gone silent, waiting to see what the king's messenger would do.

"Do you know what this badge means?" asked the king's messenger, pointing to the crest sewn onto the breast of his dark tunic.

"It's the king's crest," replied Elias meekly.

"And do you know who I am?"

Elias's heart pounded in his ears and he felt his knees weaken. "The king's messenger?"

"That is exactly right. Now, do you think it is wise to question the will of the king?" The king's messenger leaned over Elias threateningly.

Elias gulped. His voice came out in a meek whisper. "No, sir."

The king's messenger stepped forward and grabbed Elias gently by the chin. Elias looked up and found himself caught by the old man's intense gaze. Now that he was so close, Elias thought the man's eyes looked like bottomless black pits. He was so terrified he couldn't even tremble.

The king's messenger released Elias after a moment and tousled his hair playfully. "Elias did not mean anything by his comment. He is just a curious boy. There is no harm done."

A sigh of relief arose from the villagers. Lucas moved over and shoved Elias roughly back toward the crowd. "That's more than enough from you, little brother," Lucas hissed under his breath. "Now get out of here!"

Elias stumbled a bit from the rough treatment, but didn't fall down. He was used to getting picked on by his big brother, but having it happen in front of the whole village and the king's messenger was terribly embarrassing. He squeezed through the crowd and ran all the way home.

CHAPTER 2

Not Who He Seems

The next morning, Elias watched Lucas pack his things for the dragon hunt. A wheel of cheese, a big loaf of dark bread, and a thick slice of ham were wrapped up in a heavy cloth and tossed into Lucas's knapsack. Lucas slung the knapsack onto his back and grabbed his long spear from the corner. Without looking at his younger brother, Lucas called out, "I'll be back in a few days with the dragon's head. Try to stay out of trouble while I'm gone." Lucas stepped out the door and slammed it behind him without a backward glance.

'What's he so upset about?' Elias thought angrily. It was a perfectly reasonable question to have asked, and Lucas was still getting his chance to be a big hero. Elias sat and thought for a while before finally deciding to go and see the village send off his brother. He was still mad, but he didn't want to miss the excitement.

The whole village was once again gathered in the Village Square to see Lucas off on his quest. Lucas climbed up onto his big horse and saluted the crowd with his spear. Everyone cheered loudly. Well, everyone except Elias. Elias was hiding behind the blacksmith's shop watching the event rather than participating. He was pretty sure his brother wouldn't want him to be there, and he was really more interested in the king's messenger anyway. There was something about the old man's nasty black eyes that made Elias uneasy.

While the rest of the villagers followed Lucas and his horse, Elias sneaked from building to building and kept his eyes on the king's messenger. Once the crowd reached the edge of the village, Lucas nudged his horse to a trot and quickly disappeared into the woods.

The king's messenger had stayed at the back of the crowd and as soon as Lucas was out of sight, he walked quickly back to the stable where he had left his horse. Elias carefully and quietly sneaked around the side of the stable and peered through the open door. He watched the king's messenger approach a horse with a saddle in his hands but the horse shied away in terror, its eyes wide open.

"Stupid animal!" Elias heard the king's messenger say. "Keep still!"

The horse wanted nothing to do with the king's messenger though. The frightened horse thrashed from side to side. With an exasperated sigh, the king's messenger tossed the saddle aside and spread his arms wide. Elias was expecting him to try and reassure the horse the way he had seen Lucas work with bad-tempered animals. Instead, the king's messenger lowered his head and began to chant in a low, nasty voice. The air between the messenger's hands started to glow. Elias's eyes opened wide as he watched the king's messenger gesture toward the frightened horse.

Immediately, the animal stopped trembling and stood perfectly still.

'*A wizard!*' Elias thought. '*The old man is not the king's messenger but a creepy wizard!*' Elias was shocked. He had heard all kinds of stories about wizards - and all of them scared him a lot. Wizards were very scary people that used magic spells to burn things up or make people do whatever they wanted.

"That's better," said the wizard to the horse, "but I think my spells aren't working very well against you anymore. It will be time for a new horse very soon." The old man laughed evilly as he threw his saddle onto the animal's back.

Elias turned away from the stable door and ran as fast as his legs could carry him. His brother had been tricked by a wizard! The whole village had been tricked by a wizard! What could he do? He needed to tell someone right away!

The crowd of villagers had spread out by now, but there were still a few people standing around talking. Elias saw the Mayor standing with a few other grownups and he ran toward them. "The king's messenger is a fake!" he called out hoarsely, afraid the wizard might hear him.

"What are you talking about, Elias?" snapped the Mayor.

"He's a wizard! I saw him casting a spell on his horse in the stable!" gasped Elias.

"That's ridiculous," replied the Mayor angrily. "You mustn't say such things! You'll get the whole village in trouble if you start saying bad things about the king's messenger."

"But he's not the king's messenger! He's a fake!" pleaded Elias. Just then, he saw that the wizard was coming out of the stable with his horse.

The Mayor grabbed Elias roughly by the arm. "That's quite enough," the Mayor said sternly. "The king's messenger has brought an important opportunity to the village, and I won't have you ruining it with another of your silly stories. Now, run along and don't you dare speak about him again." The other grownups nodded in agreement and looked disapprovingly at Elias.

Elias glanced over at the fake messenger, then quickly turned away. As soon as the wizard was out of sight, Elias ran all the way back to the hut he shared with his brother. While he ran, he thought about what he should do. Lucas was on a quest for an evil wizard. He was in danger! Elias was the only one who could rescue him. He would just have to chase his brother and warn him before something terrible happened.

Elias burst through the door of his hut and scrambled around to gather the things he would need. A few minutes later, he was back out the door and running towards the woods where Lucas had ridden.

CHAPTER **3**

Lost

E lias found Lucas's tracks without too much trouble.
It had rained only a few days earlier and Lucas's

horse had left big, deep prints in the soft ground. Elias kept

running for as long as he could, but after a while, he started

to get a cramp in his side and his breath came in harsh

gasps. He slowed down and stopped for a quick rest on a big

rock beside the dirt road. He looked ahead at Lucas's trail

and noticed that it left the road about 30 paces from where

he was sitting. Elias gulped. He loved playing in the woods

near the village, but this was different. All of the kids in the village told stories about the fierce animals and monsters that lived in the woods out here.

Elias got up from the rock and walked slowly to the place where Lucas's tracks went off the road. The tracks followed a small trail that twisted and turned through the thick trees and bushes. The branches and leaves drooped down and blocked out most of the sun, casting the twisty trail in darkness. Elias picked up a stone and threw it toward the dark twisting trail but he could not see where the stone fell. He hesitated to go into the dark twisty trail but figured if Lucas went in then, well, he would just have to be brave. His brother needed him!

Elias took another deep breath to slow down his racing heart and stepped off the road onto the trail.

Elias followed the trail for hours. It led down into small valleys, through creeks and over fallen trees. It was hard, but Elias didn't even think about giving up. Well, at least not until he heard a loud rustling noise.

His heart leaped into his throat and he froze in his tracks. He slowly turned toward the sound and strained his eyes in the dim light to see what might have caused it. His mind raced through all the stories he had heard from the other children. Could it be a bear? A mountain lion? Then another thought popped into his mind: The dragon! What if he ran into the dragon? Lucas might be able to slay a dragon with his great spear, but what was Elias going to do? He looked down at his small eating dagger and shook his head. He had left the village so quickly he hadn't thought things through. All he wanted to do was help his brother and now he was probably going to be the one who needed help!

"Calm down," he told himself. He took a deep breath and forced himself to look carefully in the direction of the crashing sound and saw... a squirrel. It jumped from one low-hanging tree branch to another, and the leaves rustled loudly against each other. Elias couldn't help but laugh out loud. He turned around and started down the trail again.

It wasn't long before his stomach growled loudly to remind him that he hadn't eaten since early in the morning, so Elias decided to stop for dinner. Not far from the trail was a fallen tree that made a great bench. He sat down and opened his lunch. It was amazing how good a piece of hard cheese and bread could taste.

As he ate, Elias watched the sun going down. He had always loved sunsets. His enjoyment was interrupted very soon though, when he realized what else sunset meant. It was going to be night soon. He was going to be sitting in the middle of the forest, on his own, in the dark. *'Why, oh why didn't I think this through before I left home?'* he thought.

It had taken him all day to get here, so it was way too late to try and get back to the village.

As the sun kept creeping down below the trees, shadows began to stretch out and form nasty-looking shapes across the ground. Elias packed up what was left of his dinner and set off down the trail. If it was getting dark, Lucas would also have to make camp soon. Elias would just have to keep going until he found him.

As the forest grew darker and darker, Elias found himself tripping and stumbling more and more often. Though he couldn't see them, he could feel that his pants were getting torn by branches and bushes as he pushed along the trail. His arms were getting scratched up too, and it was getting colder by the minute. All the sounds of the forest got louder and scarier. Elias felt miserable. All he wanted was to be back in his little hut in the village with a nice fire burning in the fireplace. His tired body ached for the nice comfy feeling of warm blankets.

Elias was imagining that comfy feeling and didn't notice when the trail dropped away in front of him. One moment he was walking along, and the next thing he knew he was tumbling down a steep hill. He banged into trees and bounced off rocks, then slid to a stop. It took him a minute to gather his senses. When he did, the first thing he realized was that he had dropped his knapsack during his fall. He looked around, but it was so dark he could hardly see his hand held up in front of him. There was no way he could find his knapsack. The situation seemed so hopeless that Elias started to cry. It was only one tear at first, but soon his whole body was shaking with sobs.

CHAPTER 4

The Dragon

After a few minutes of crying, Elias sat up slowly and stretched out each of his arms and legs, just to make sure he could move them. When he was sure he hadn't broken any of his bones, he looked around in the dark to try and figure out where he had landed. In the dark, he could not see much but he could hear the sound of running water. Below him he could feel cold mud squishing between his fingers. He must have fallen by a stream.

A bit ashamed of his crying, Elias crawled toward the water sound. He splashed some water onto his face and tried to clean some of the mud off. While he was doing that, a flash of light caught his eye. The light was coming from upstream.

Now that he was aware of it, Elias could see that it didn't actually flash and go away completely. Instead it flared up brightly for a moment, then slowly faded away. Despite being wet, cold, dirty and scared, the light gave Elias something to think about and, in a strange way, it made him feel a bit better. *'It must be Lucas!'* he thought.

Elias started carefully picking his way past the big rocks and upstream toward the light. As he got closer to the source of the light, Elias started to hear a strange sound coming from the same direction. It was a deep, rumbling sound that carried over the noise of the stream and it somehow made Elias feel a little sad. Curious, he kept moving toward it.

The next time the light flared up, Elias could see that it was coming from between two huge rocks.

As he approached a little closer, he realized the light was

actually coming from a cave behind the rocks.

Maybe this is where Lucas made his camp. But what could Lucas be doing to make that noise?

Unsure but hopeful, Elias crept as silently as he could to the mouth of the cave. He crouched down by one of the huge rocks and, ever so slowly, he peeked around it. What he saw almost made his heart stop.

A dragon!

Elias trembled in terror and tried to press himself into the rock. The light wasn't Lucas's campfire. It was the dragon's fiery breath! It must be roasting something. Or someone!

Elias desperately looked around and tried to think of something he could do to avoid being the next thing the dragon roasted. His only idea was to sneak away and hope with all his heart that whatever was making the sad noise would keep the dragon from hearing him.

Then it occurred to him. What was the sad noise? It seemed to be coming from the cave. It wasn't a noise he

thought a dragon would make. In fact, it sounded a lot like...
crying.

Elias froze in fear at the thought that the crying might actually be his brother. Had Lucas been caught by the dragon? Curiosity and fear battled back and forth in Elias's mind until, finally, curiosity won. He peered around the rock again, and this time he looked at the dragon more carefully.

It was about as big as the huge horses Farmer Brown used on his farm. It had dark green scales over most of its body and red spines ran from above its eyes down its long neck to the tip of its tail. Just as he got a good look at the beast, Elias peeked over to try to get a better look around the cave for his brother. Elias was almost blinded as the dragon let out another bright blast of fiery breath. After hours in the dark, the bright light left stars and spots dancing in Elias's eyes. Elias ducked back behind the rock and shut his eyes tightly until the spots went away.

It took a few moments for Elias's vision to return to normal.

The dragon hadn't eaten him during that time, so Elias figured the dragon hadn't noticed him.

The dragon's fiery breath continued to light up the area once in a while followed by the sad sound of crying. He had not seen Lucas nor his horse in the cave. But, if it was Lucas crying, then he was still alive. Elias had to do something to save his brother from the dragon.

Elias crouched as low as he could behind the huge rock and tried to figure out what to do next. Well, what were his options? He couldn't run away and leave his brother. Besides, if he tried running away, he'd probably just trip on something and the dragon would hear and it would come and eat him. If he stayed where he was, the dragon would eventually come out of its cave and eat him. If he went into the cave, the dragon would probably eat him. Hmmm... none of those options sounded very good. He sat and thought for a bit longer, then decided. He was cold and wet and dirty and miserable. And that could be his brother crying for help in there.

There was no way he could find his way to the village to get help in the dark and, no matter what he did, it seemed like he was going to be eaten by a dragon. *'Might as well get it over with quickly,'* he thought.

CHAPTER 5

Facing Rhyssofol

Elias took a deep breath, stood up, and called out in a loud, clear voice. "Hey, Dragon! Let my brother go!"

The dragon moved so fast that Elias just saw it as a blur. One moment it was lying in its cave, and the next it had leaped over the huge rock and pinned him to it with a long, powerful arm. As the dragon's claws tightened around his chest, Elias was sure he was about to die. A single frightened tear slid down his cheek as he squeezed his eyes shut and waited to be eaten.

Instead of feeling teeth biting into him, Elias felt the

dragon's grip loosen. He heard a low, hoarse voice and opened his eyes in amazement. The dragon was talking to him.

"Who are you? Why are you hunting me?" asked the dragon. The voice sounded old and dignified, and Elias somehow knew it was female.

Elias saw the dragon's face hovering right in front of him. He gulped. "I'm not hunting anyone. I'm just trying to find my brother. Please don't hurt me."

"Sneaky little human-thing. Are you telling me lies?" demanded the dragon angrily. Despite the angry words, it loosened its grip a little more and moved its head away from him. Elias had been right about it being the size of Farmer Brown's horses. What he hadn't noticed before was the creature's wings. They were twice as big as the rest of its body and right now they flared out behind it like an enormous tent.

"I'm not lying. I promise. I don't want to hurt you. I just

want to find my brother and go home," Elias stammered.

"Well, your brother isn't here," the dragon said.

Elias was relieved to hear that but he was also confused. "I heard crying," he said and quickly realized that the crying was coming from the dragon herself as he saw her red teary eyes.

"My mother told me humans couldn't be trusted. Small but clever she always said." The dragon cocked her head to the side as if she was thinking very hard about something. "Too clever to send such a little one with no metal skin or sharp stick." The dragon let Elias go and stepped back. She coiled her enormous wings back around her body the way they had been when Elias first saw her.

"I beg your pardon, Miss Dragon, ma'am," said Elias. "What are you going to do with me?"

The dragon tossed her head back and forth irritably. "I do not know yet," she replied.

Now that the dragon had let him go, Elias felt a bit less afraid.

In fact, now that his chances of being eaten seemed so much smaller, his curiosity started to get the better of him again. He watched the starlight glint off the dragon's scales as she moved her head and neck back and forth in a swaying motion. She was really quite a beautiful creature - when she wasn't trying to eat you.

"Why were you crying?" Elias asked abruptly.

The dragon whipped her head back around in front of him. For a moment, she didn't reply. "I did not think humans knew about crying," she said. "When is it that you cry?"

"We cry when we are sad," Elias replied. "Or sometimes when we're very happy."

The dragon cocked her head to the side again. "I was crying because I am sad," she said, after a moment. Elias had trouble imagining what would make such a magnificent and powerful creature sad enough to cry. "I am sad because a human has stolen my baby," she added, her wings flaring out slightly.

"I'm very sorry to hear that," said Elias. "Do you know which human took your baby?"

"I do not know his name, but I know that he is a powerful wizard," replied the dragon.

Elias gasped. "A bad wizard came to my village and offered a reward for a dragon's head!" he exclaimed without thinking. "It must be the same wizard that took your baby!"

"A reward for my head?!" snapped the dragon. "You said you were not hunting me!" Her wings flared out to full size, and one of her massive clawed feet reached for Elias.

"No! I wasn't hunting you, I promise! I'm looking for my brother, like I said." The dragon's claws closed around Elias and squeezed so tight his breath came out in a whoosh.

"And what is your brother doing wandering in the woods at night?" she demanded, squeezing Elias even tighter. "Is he the one with the metal skin and sharp stick?"

Elias tried to reply, but there was no breath left in his lungs. Instead he made a sort of grunting, wheezing noise and felt himself start to get light-headed. The dragon held him for a moment longer then let go. Elias collapsed to the ground, gasping for air.

After taking a few deep breaths, he looked up at the angry creature looming over him. "My brother doesn't know he is a bad wizard. He just wants to be a hero."

"By killing a dragon?" shouted the dragon angrily. "It is just as my mother taught me. Humans are good for nothing. Not even eating!"

The dragon raised her big foot over Elias and prepared to stomp him. Elias closed his eyes and cringed, waiting to be squished into the rocks below him. But he noticed the dragon hesitating. It was as if the dragon didn't really want to kill him.

"Wait!" Elias yelled. "I can help you get your baby back from the wizard!"

Elias felt the dragon's claws close around his chest again and he gasped as the dragon picked him up.

"How can you do that?" she asked suspiciously.

Elias wondered the same thing. What could he possibly do against a wizard? His mind raced. "We can find my brother and he'll help us!" he exclaimed. "Lucas is the biggest, strongest person in the village. If anyone could beat the wizard, it's him."

The dragon snorted and small blasts of flame lit up the darkness. "Strength is nothing against a wizard. One spell and your brother will think he is the wizard's best friend," said the dragon.

Despite what she said, the dragon didn't squeeze Elias this time. "There must be some way I can help," he said.

The dragon frowned at Elias and he felt her anger in his head along with her words. "The last time I trusted a human, I woke to find my baby missing."

Something about the dragon's words stuck in Elias's head. "Why..." he began, then paused. "If the wizard wanted to kill you," he continued, "why didn't he do it while you were sleeping? Why didn't he throw fireballs or bolts of lightning or something? And why did he have to wait for you to sleep if he could use a spell to make you think he was your friend?"

"First, a wizard's magic cannot affect a dragon's mind. Second, this wizard cannot throw fireballs or bolts of lightning, I don't think. And he is too weak to pierce my scales, even while I am sleeping," replied the dragon.

"Then why can't you get your baby back from him? Is it hidden?" asked Elias.

The dragon snarled. "He has taken my baby to his tower

and locked it in a cell in the basement. The tower is made of solid black stones and I am too big to get inside the small doorway or go down to the basement."

Elias thought about that for a minute. "If the door is too small for a big dragon, maybe a little boy could get in."

The dragon went completely still for a moment, then starlight twinkled off her teeth as her mouth widened in a grin. "Maybe you can help after all," she said. "My name is Rhyssofol, but you may call me Rhys."

"I am Elias," replied the young boy.

The dragon did not look scary any more. "Come into my cave and be warm," she said. "In the morning, we will go hunting for a wizard!"

CHAPTER 6

Unexpected Visitor

Elias awoke to bright sun in his eyes. He had a moment of panic at first because he couldn't remember where he was. Everything came flooding back, though, as he looked up to see the dragon's shadow block out the sun as it entered the cave he had slept the night in.

"Is this yours?" asked Rhys as she dropped a tattered cloth bag in front of Elias.

"My bag!" Elias leapt to his feet, ignoring the stiffness in his muscles from sleeping on the hard ground. His excitement faded a bit when he picked up the sack. There was a big tear in the side and the food he had brought was all missing. His stomach growled with hunger and his temper flared. "Did you eat my food?" he asked accusingly. "I would have shared if you had asked."

Rhys snorted and the spines on her back rose up. "I have no need for your food. Dragons only eat once a week."

"I'm sorry," said Elias. "I didn't mean to be rude. I'm just not quite awake yet I think."

The spines on the dragon's back settled down, and she made a noise Elias thought might be a chuckle. "You are just like my baby - always grumpy in the mornings. How does your mother cope with you?"

Elias sat down quietly. "I don't have a mother... or a father... they both died when I was very young."

Rhys cocked her head to the side curiously. "I do not understand human ways, but you seem quite small to live alone," she said.

"I don't live alone," replied Elias. "My brother takes care

of me. He always has."

Before Elias could say more, a loud voice thundered down the small valley. "Get away from him!" yelled the voice. Elias and Rhys turned to the source of the call and saw a large man on an even larger horse charging toward them with his spear aimed straight at the dragon. It was Lucas!

Rhys flared her wings out to their full size and whirled to face Lucas's charge. Elias watched in horror as his brother tucked his boar-spear tight under his arm and prepared to slam into the dragon. Rhys had other ideas, however. With a single flap of her wings she leaped into the air and up over Lucas and his horse. As she passed over them, she lashed out with one of her powerful legs and knocked Lucas out of his saddle. He tumbled roughly to the ground and his spear went flying.

Elias yelled and ran to his brother. Lucas was not out of the fight yet, and he drew his long knife as he rolled to his feet. The dragon let out a terrible hissing noise, and Elias felt her voice echo in his head. "Get away from him, Elias, or my breath will roast you too!"

"No!" screamed Elias. "He's my brother. You can't hurt him!"

Rhys reared back angrily but didn't attack. Instead she turned and roared at Lucas's terrified horse, sending it galloping away.

Lucas extended his blade toward the dragon and held an arm out in front of Elias protectively. "Get behind me," Lucas said.

Elias looked from his brother to the massive beast looming over them and wondered at how only yesterday he had thought Lucas was invincible. Compared to the dragon though, he seemed pitifully small and weak. "Please!" he cried. "Stop fighting!"

"What are you saying?" demanded Lucas. "This beast was about to kill you!"

"No, Lucas, you don't understand. Rhys is my friend. I'm going to help her get her baby back," shouted Elias.

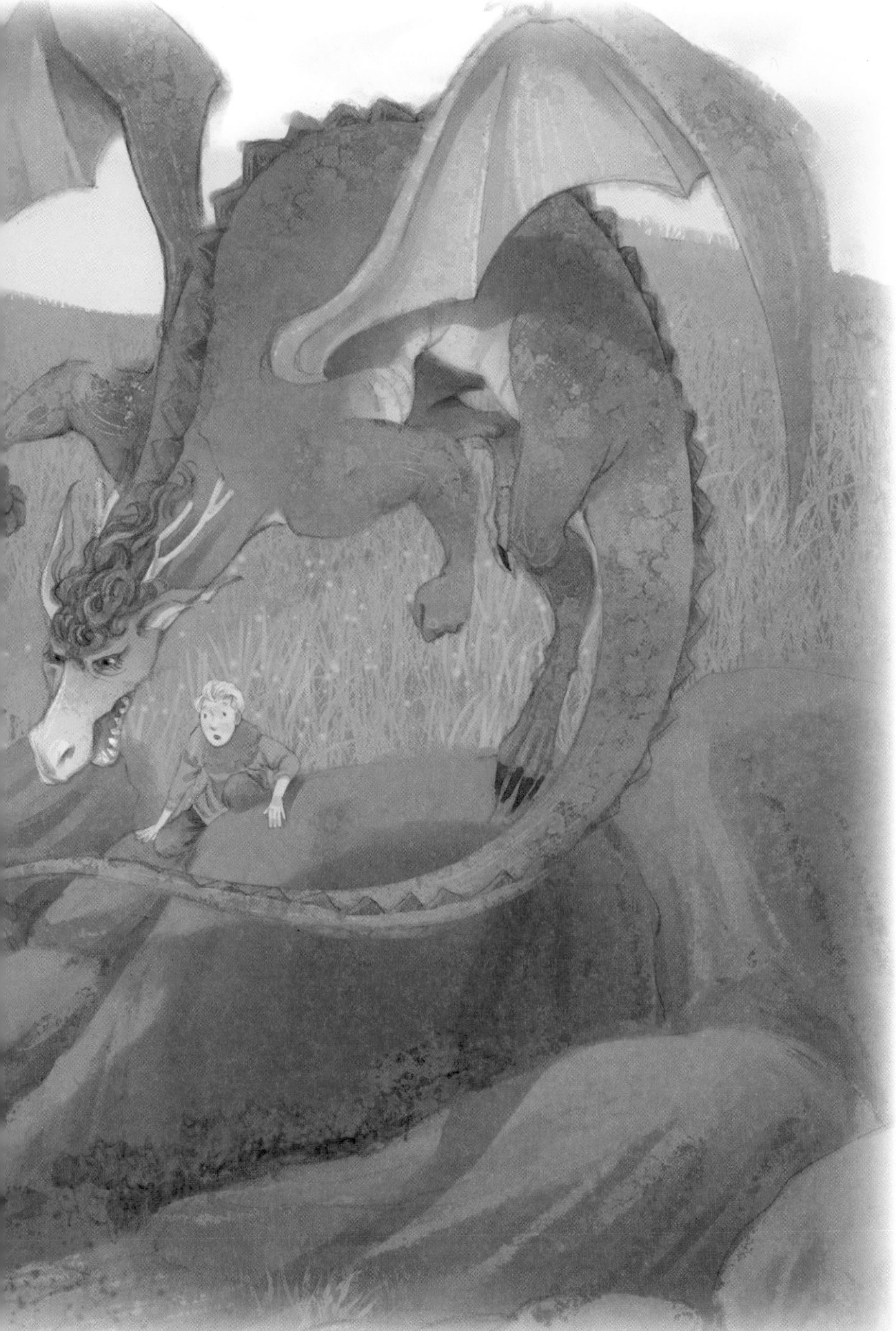

Lucas took his eyes off of the dragon to look at Elias. "You made friends with a dragon?" Before Elias could respond, Rhys lashed out with a claw and knocked Lucas's knife from his hand. The blade skipped loudly along the rocks and came to a rest a few dozen meters away.

"She's not bad," Elias replied. "She just wants her baby back." He gently pushed Lucas's arm down and stepped between him and the dragon. "I told her we could help."

Lucas took several steps back, nearly tripping on the rocky terrain. "Dragons eat people! This thing is tricking you."

"I would never eat a human," said Rhys disgustedly. "And I don't need trickery to beat the likes of you!" She raised a huge clawed foot menacingly.

Lucas scrambled further away and looked angrily at Elias. "You are betraying your own people. You're no brother of mine!" He turned and raced away.

Rhys snarled and started to chase, but Elias called her back. "Please don't," he pleaded. He hung his head sadly. "Just let him go."

"This is the way human brothers treat each other?" asked Rhys. "Even worse than my mother told me."

"I think he's just embarrassed," said Elias. "He's usually the hero, not the one getting rescued. Anyway, it doesn't matter. I promised I would help you get your baby back and I will. Let's get started."

CHAPTER 7

To the Tower

E lias clung tightly to the spines on Rhys's back as the wind screamed past him. The treetops sped by a few meters below. He was flying!

"We're almost there," said the dragon. Elias nodded his head but didn't bother to reply. The wind was so loud he was sure his voice wouldn't carry anyway.

Rhys turned sharply and started to descend. A moment later, they landed softly on the open ground near the tower. Elias slipped off her back and tried to calm his racing heart.

"I'm sorry if the trip was rough," said Rhys. "I've never

carried anyone before."

"It was amazing!" said Elias. "Dragons are so lucky!"

"We will need more than luck today, I'm afraid," she replied sadly.

Elias reached out and touched her arm. "I'll get your baby back," he said, with more confidence than he felt.

"I'll wait behind the trees for you," she said. "Good luck."

Elias turned and stared at the tall black tower. He guessed it must be 10 stories high. It was made from dark stones that seemed to soak up the sunlight and it cast the whole area in shadow. Elias walked slowly toward the tower. With each step he fully expected a bolt of lightning or a ball of fire to come down and burn him up. Instead, he reached the stone wall unharmed. Perhaps Rhys was right - the wizard couldn't make fireballs or lightning bolts. Well, hopefully that would make the job easier. Elias edged around the base of the tower, searching for the door. The strange shadows and dark stones around the tower made it hard, but he eventually found the spot. It was a small wooden door that had been painted black to match the rest of the building. Elias pulled on the handle and, to his surprise, it swung open without a sound.

Though the tower blocked sunlight from coming in, the inside was dimly lit by a source Elias couldn't see yet. He clenched his fists and tried to feel brave as he stepped into the small room beyond the doorway. Three more closed doors, one on each wall, were the only features of the room. Not at all sure where to go, Elias randomly chose the door on the right and opened it. Behind the door, a stairway led

upwards. This couldn't be the right door because Rhys had

said that her baby was kept in a cell in the basement. Elias

opened the next door, and that led into a broom closet. He

wondered if one of those brooms was a magic flying broom,

but decided not to try. Elias finally opened the third door

and saw a stairway leading downwards. This must be it.

Damp, smelly air wafted into Elias's nose. Well, a bad smell

was hardly the worst thing he had encountered. He slowly

and carefully walked down the stairs after closing the door

behind him.

Elias hadn't even reached the bottom step when he heard

a sad noise. He peered around the corner and saw a large

metal door. Behind the door sat a baby dragon! It was about

half his size. Elias couldn't believe his luck. This was going to

be easy!

A look around the room reminded him he still needed to be

careful. It might be a baby, but it could still breathe fire.

The walls, floor and even the ceiling of the room showed scorch marks from the dragon's breath. He called out to it softly. "Hello. I'm here to rescue you. Your mother, Rhyssofol, sent me." The dragon's head whipped up to face him. It looked suspicious, but it stayed silent. On a hook on the opposite side of the room hung a ring of large metal keys. "Those must be for the lock on your door," Elias said, as he walked cautiously across the room. Elias reached for the keys when he heard a voice behind him.

"Do you have any idea what I do with thieves, little boy?"

Elias was so startled he nearly jumped. He whirled around to see the hunched figure of the wizard standing at the bottom of the stairs.

"Did you really think you could just walk in here and steal from me?" The wizard extended his arm, spoke a few strange words and pointed.

Elias felt something grip the back of his head, and his brain started to feel fuzzy. The wizard crooked his finger and, though he tried his hardest not to, Elias found himself walking across the room and coming to a stop in front of the wizard.

"That's a good boy," cackled the old man. "You look strong and healthy. Perhaps I won't feed you to my new pet. I've been thinking about getting a servant for some time now." He cackled again.

Elias struggled against the grip on his brain, but it was no use. The best he could manage was to close his eyes.

"Now, now. No need to be afraid. I think we'll be friends," said the wizard in a nasty voice. Elias could feel another spell start to work on his mind. He fought against it, but soon he couldn't remember what he was fighting against. Before his eyes, the old man's nasty, wrinkled face grew smoother and nicer looking. Elias thought he had never seen a kinder, more generous person in his whole life.

'Wait! This isn't right!' Elias shook his head from side to side.

"My, my… you have a very strong mind," said the wizard.
"This may take a minute." Before he could begin speaking a
new spell, however, the wizard let out a yelp and leaped
back. Elias felt the grip on his mind loosen and he saw that
the baby dragon had blasted the old man with its fiery
breath. Before the wizard could recover, Elias jumped
forward and kicked him in the shin as hard as he could. The
old man yelped again, and Elias pushed past him and ran
up the stairs.

Elias burst through the door at the top of the stairs and received yet another surprise. Lucas was standing in the middle of the small room holding a large wooden club. Instead of saying hello, he gestured wildly at Elias to get out of the way. Elias dove to the ground and rolled away as Lucas stepped forward and brought the club down on the wizard's head with a smack. The old man tumbled back down the stairs and collapsed in a heap.

"I thought you might need some help, little brother," said Lucas with a smile. Elias didn't say a word. He just hugged his brother with all of his strength. "Hey now, don't squish me," said Lucas. "We're not out of this yet. We still have a baby dragon to rescue."

EPILOGUE

"Elias was right," said Lucas to the Mayor. "That was no king's messenger. He was an evil wizard." Elias and Lucas were back in the village sitting at the big table in the Mayor's house. Elias had never been here before, but he knew this was where important people in the village came to talk about important things. "And the dragon is no threat to us," continued Lucas. "In fact, she has offered to make her home near the village so we can help protect each other. That may not be a hundred gold pieces, but it's a pretty good prize."

"I suppose I owe you an apology, young man," said the Mayor. "And everyone in Gallive owes you their thanks. Would it be alright if I met this dragon now?"

Elias nodded proudly. "She's with her baby just outside the village. We didn't want to scare anyone."

A few minutes later they stood in front of the dragon. The Mayor's eyes widened as Rhys stood up. Elias wondered how he would react if she spread her wings. Instead, she bowed her head low. "Sir Mayor, this is the dragon Rhyssofol," said Elias.

"It is a great honor," said the Mayor solemnly, "to welcome you to the village of Gallive."